BACKSTREET BOYS

USA

ATLANTA 1996
TM.© 1992 ACOG

OMNIBUS PRESS

They call Florida the Sunshine State – and The Backstreet Boys, five young men from America's holiday haven, certainly live up to that label. Their infectious harmonies, hook-filled songs and, last but not least, clean-cut good looks have marked them out among the shoal of Nineties boy bands as leaders in the field. And even in the depths of a British winter, their sunny sound warmed the lives of thousands as the charts resounded to the Backstreet beat.

America, of course, is where the boy band was invented. Remember The Jackson Five and The Osmonds in the Seventies? Your mum will! Since then, we've had the likes of New Kids On The Block and New Edition, from which Bobby Brown found solo fame, not to mention East 17, Boyzone, 3T and the other stars of today. But The Backstreet Boys have made their own unique mark as five individual personalities – each loveable in his own right – whose whole is greater than the sum of the parts. When those five voices blend together, then you can be sure musical magic is in the air!

But where did it all begin? The story begins not with Nick, Brian, Kevin, Howard or AJ but Lou J Pearlman, the cousin of Sixties singing star Art Garfunkel, whose concept The Backstreet Boys was. Howie credited him on their album as being his friend, teacher and adviser on life – and that's quite some compliment! Brian, who calls him Big Poppa, simply says: "If it wasn't for your dreams, our dreams wouldn't be possible." Between the five (or should that be six?) of them they've made many millions more dreams come true in the two years they've been together.

The management team of Donna and Johnny Wright had steered the New Kids On The Block to fame and fortune just a few years earlier and were looking to repeat the feat with a new and equally talented team. The call went out to audition, as happens in these cases, and though they'd seen it all before, even the Wrights were amazed at the combination they came up with. Oldest of the crew was Kentucky-born Kevin Richardson, a strapping six-footer who could play the piano as well as sing. He was no stranger to role-playing either, having worked at Walt Disney World as both Aladdin and a Teenage Mutant Ninja Turtle!

Next up was Howard Dorough, Howie D to his friends and the first of two Florida natives in the band. He is nearly a year younger than Kev, and his background included commercials, musical theatre and voice-overs. The pair had met when competing for a $1000 prize in a talent contest: they had to stage a totally original 45-minute show in which they sang, danced and acted. "Of course I went out and blew all the money!" says Kev, the victor on that occasion. "You would, wouldn't you?"

Third oldest was Brian Littrell, Kev's cousin and a sporty type who earned his nickname B-Rock "because I like to play basketball." A big fan of black R&B, especially velvet-voiced Luther Vandross, he'd squeezed a whole Yellow Pages' worth of jobs into his teenage years, from a fast-food assistant at a burger bar to a wedding co-ordinator – the person who organises everything. When the chance to audition came up, he'd been in his history class at school, and was pulled out to take Kev's call. Next day he was on a plane to Orlando... and the rest is history!

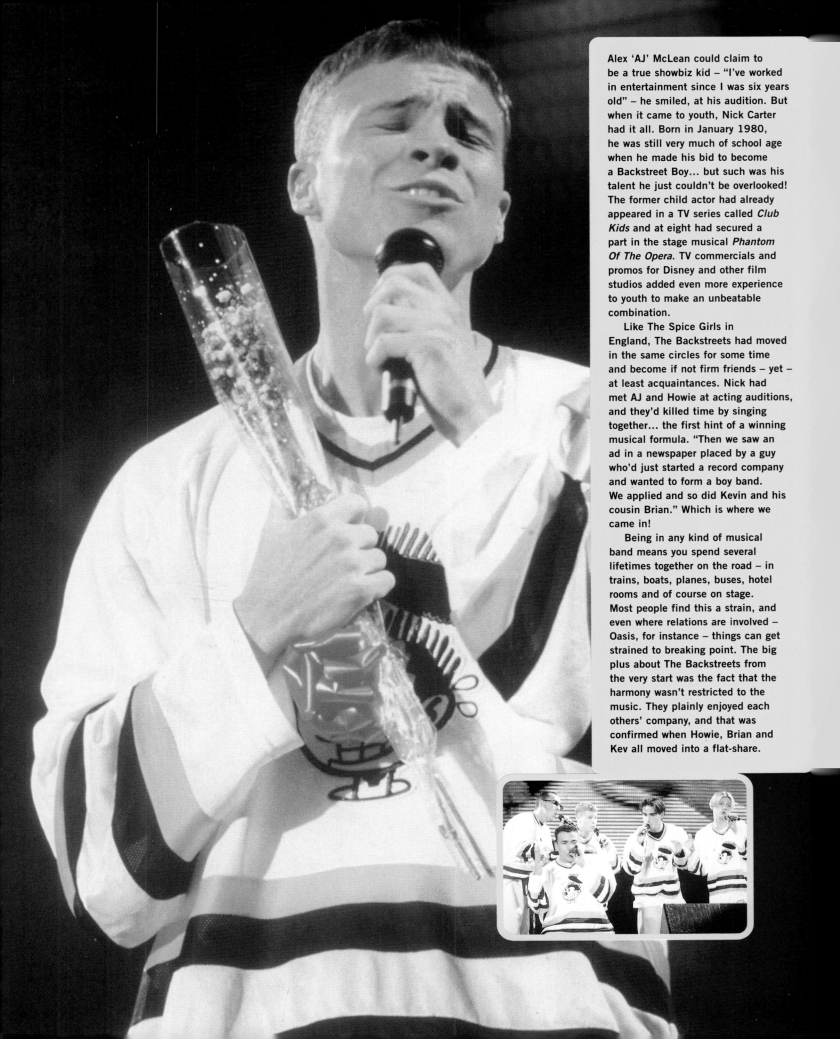

Alex 'AJ' McLean could claim to be a true showbiz kid – "I've worked in entertainment since I was six years old" – he smiled, at his audition. But when it came to youth, Nick Carter had it all. Born in January 1980, he was still very much of school age when he made his bid to become a Backstreet Boy... but such was his talent he just couldn't be overlooked! The former child actor had already appeared in a TV series called *Club Kids* and at eight had secured a part in the stage musical *Phantom Of The Opera*. TV commercials and promos for Disney and other film studios added even more experience to youth to make an unbeatable combination.

Like The Spice Girls in England, The Backstreets had moved in the same circles for some time and become if not firm friends – yet – at least acquaintances. Nick had met AJ and Howie at acting auditions, and they'd killed time by singing together... the first hint of a winning musical formula. "Then we saw an ad in a newspaper placed by a guy who'd just started a record company and wanted to form a boy band. We applied and so did Kevin and his cousin Brian." Which is where we came in!

Being in any kind of musical band means you spend several lifetimes together on the road – in trains, boats, planes, buses, hotel rooms and of course on stage. Most people find this a strain, and even where relations are involved – Oasis, for instance – things can get strained to breaking point. The big plus about The Backstreets from the very start was the fact that the harmony wasn't restricted to the music. They plainly enjoyed each others' company, and that was confirmed when Howie, Brian and Kev all moved into a flat-share.

Togetherness would quickly become a BSB watchword, to the point that Brian claimed if anyone went solo "It wouldn't be The Backstreet Boys any more... everybody's a major part."

The signs were there early on that The Backstreet Boys were going to be huge – but the one surprise was that it happened in Europe before they cracked it in their native US of A. Germany would be first to send their début album to platinum status, and in Spain they were mobbed and had their jewellery torn from their still-quaking bods! But all this was still to come of course when they stepped into a recording studio to cut their first music together. The blend had sounded great in rehearsal, but would the magic translate onto recording tape? Five Boys held their breath...

But they needn't have worried. The magic formula more or less wrote itself in the first three tracks to be cut, though each was very different and recorded in a different place. 'We've Got It Goin' On', the song that would eventually lead off their first album, was a stomping dance cut, recorded and produced in Sweden by Denniz Pop. In total contrast, 'I'll Never Break Your Heart' was a creamy-smooth ballad which they recorded close to home in Orlando, Florida, and which contained all the sunshine of their native State, while 'Roll With It' – absolutely no relation to the Oasis song! – was committed to tape in downtown Chicago. It was a song with a message, Nick revealed: "If you feel no-one cares, then hang in there and it'll get better." It certainly would...

With three potential smash singles under their belt, the Boys decided to hit the road, and though 'We've Got It Goin' On' (at No.54) would fail to make the breakthrough in Britain, the Boys ventured to Europe for the first time in the summer of 1995. Touring with PJ and Duncan, they made an immediate impression. Such an impact, in fact, that they were voted *Smash Hits*' Best Newcomers of the year. Indeed Gavin Reeve, who reviewed 'We've Got It... ' pronounced it "catchier than the fearsome cold that's going round our office", giving it a five-star rating. He's now the magazine's editor, which says much for his taste and perception!

With that magazine's backing, everything was set up for 'I'll Never Break Your Heart' to write the Backstreet name all over the airwaves. The perfect showcase for those trademark harmonies, it obliged by doing the business, breaking into the chart at No. 3. With 'We've Got It Goin' On' re-released in Britain and a hit second time round, the likes of Boyzone, Take That and East 17 were busy looking over their shoulders at a new name coming up on the outside. The only setback was Kevin contracting appendicitis on tour, which meant performing some dates as a four-piece while he recovered from his emergency op!

It was time for the band to release their first album, which naturally enough took their name as its title. Many different writers and producers contributed their talents to the result: 'Darlin'', for instance, was written and produced by Timmy Allen, a man best-known for his work with black music giant R Kelly and teen sensation Aaliyah. The bouncy 'Boys Will Be Boys', a kind of signature tune for the fivesome, was scheduled to make the soundtrack of not one but two movies – Eddie Murphy's remake of *The Nutty Professor*, and a basketball flick featuring sports superstar Shaquille O'Neal.

And as 1996 turned into 1997, the singles still kept on coming. 'Quit Playing Games With My Heart' got to No. 2 in the charts, held off the top by American songstress Tori Amos.

'Anywhere For You' appeared in March and even though it was now nearly two years' old, showed its class by powering to No. 4. Its message, said Howie, was even more relevant now. "It talks about how we've travelled all around the world... we'll go anywhere for our fans."

And that's exactly what they did! But Britain, it seemed, held a particularly warm place in their affections. "We get really excited when we're flying back to Britain," Brian admits, "because we get to see our fans again." As for Nick, he simply smiles and says "Girls from Britain are so beautiful... "

Whiling away the hours between shows on tour can be a bore. But Brian and Nick are best buddies despite the five-year age difference: they call each other Frick and Frack, and Brian rates the youngster "The little brother I never had. I taught him how to play basketball and got him hooked on Nintendo." But as for hints on how to date girls, "we don't really talk about them." AJ admits to outrageous behaviour – "chucking fruit out of hotel windows at cars to see if it hits them" – but even though he claims that "sometimes you get so bored you want to run riot for a while" somehow you can't see The Backstreet Boys trashing hotel-rooms!

But they do know how to enjoy themselves. On their travels they've crossed paths with the outrageous Outhere Brothers of 'Boom Boom Boom' fame: Kev enjoyed some wild partying with them, but no-one's revealing any more – while appearances on Top Of The Pops and other TV shows saw them rubbing shoulders with rock's top names. "I asked for Bryan Adams' autograph," Kev admits. "I'm a big fan and we'd just come out of the studio where we've been working with his producer, which was cool."

As Kev hints, there will of course be a second Backstreet Boys album – sometime! It's tentatively scheduled for the autumn of 1997, just as soon as the Famous Five have stopped orbiting the globe promoting their fabulous first effort. And judging by the commerciality of that particular offering, they could carry on taking singles from it till the cows come home!

In November 1996 they were voted the most popular band in Europe, receiving the accolade at the MTV European Music Awards from Robbie Williams. It set the seal on a year in which they'd progressed from little-known hopefuls to top dogs on the TV screen – little wonder Nick fell over the words of his acceptance speech. "This is such an honour," he stammered: let's leave it at that!

Stardom is bringing all the rewards – fame, fortune and fans – that every would-be pop idol longs for. Yet the one thing the boys would all love, a special girl to call their own, is the one thing they just can't have. Long-lasting romance isn't on the agenda when you're criss-crossing the world racking up more air miles than Richard Branson. "Our schedule is so busy that I can't find time to date or romance a girl," says Brian, who confesses "It takes me a while to get to know a girl." For Howie, neither of his last two girlfriends could cope with the demands of his career. "I respect them for being honest but it still really hurt." Still, there's hope yet: in ten years' time, Nick wants to "be married and have a baby. Or two!" Bless…

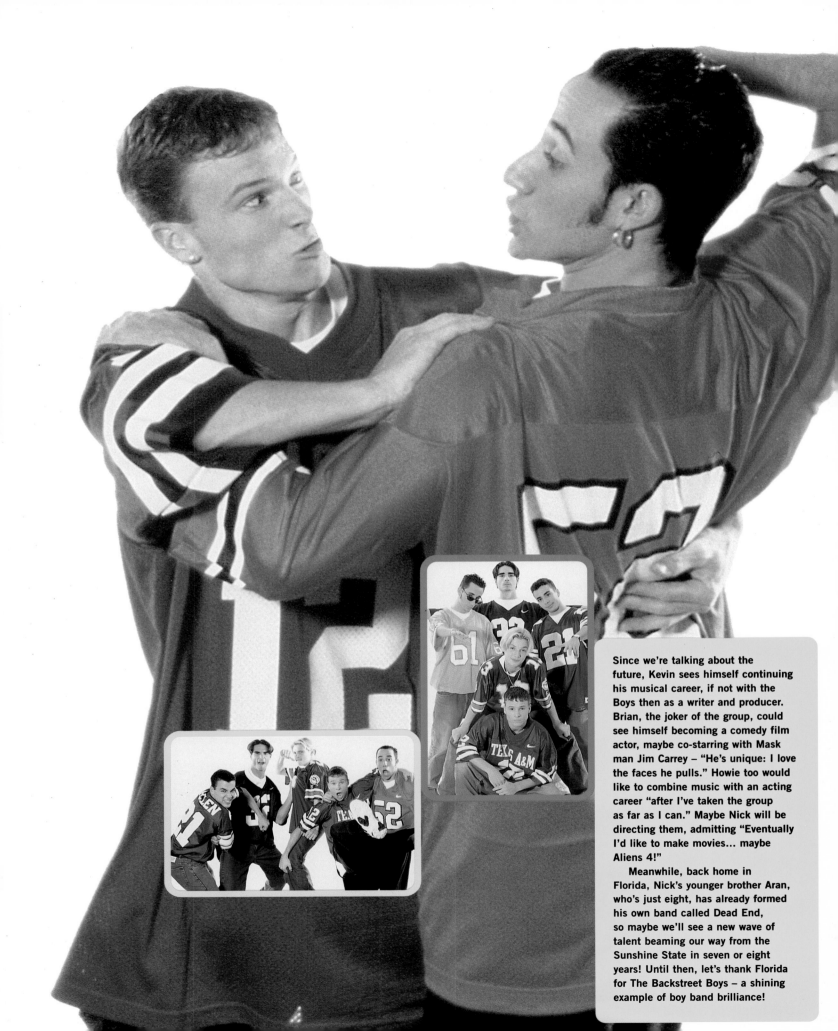

Since we're talking about the future, Kevin sees himself continuing his musical career, if not with the Boys then as a writer and producer. Brian, the joker of the group, could see himself becoming a comedy film actor, maybe co-starring with Mask man Jim Carrey – "He's unique: I love the faces he pulls." Howie too would like to combine music with an acting career "after I've taken the group as far as I can." Maybe Nick will be directing them, admitting "Eventually I'd like to make movies... maybe Aliens 4!"

Meanwhile, back home in Florida, Nick's younger brother Aran, who's just eight, has already formed his own band called Dead End, so maybe we'll see a new wave of talent beaming our way from the Sunshine State in seven or eight years! Until then, let's thank Florida for The Backstreet Boys – a shining example of boy band brilliance!

Kev

Full name: Kevin Richardson
Born: Lexington, Kentucky
Nickname: Kev
Birthdate: 3 October 1972
Zodiac sign: Libra
Height: 6' 1"
Weight: 12 stone 7 pounds
Eyes: Green
Hair: Black
Family: Mum Anne, plus two older brothers, Gerald and Tim
Heroes: Elton John and Billy Joel
Favourite things: Jewellery, especially rings
Hobbies: Playing basketball, working out
Favourite saying: 'What's up?'
Good points: Perfectionism
Bad points: Perfectionism!
Dream women?: Michelle Pfeiffer and Demi Moore
Favourite food: Mexican or Chinese
Favourite smell: XS by Paco Rabanne

AJ

Full name: Alexander James McLean
Born: South Palm Beach, Florida
Nickname: AJ or Bone
Birthdate: 9 January 1978
Zodiac sign: Capricorn
Height: 5' 9"
Weight: 9 stone
Eyes: Brown
Hair: Black
Family: Mum Denise and dad Bob (now divorced)
Heroes: An uncle who played bass in a 1950s band called Richie and the Rockets. 'He was a big influence on me even though they never made it big.'
Hobbies: Basketball and swimming
Favourite saying: "It's gonna be funky!"
Good points: A good listener when the others have problems
Bad points: Notoriously impatient – and can't keep secrets!
Dream women: Cindy Crawford and Pamela Anderson
Favourite food: McDonald's double cheeseburger meal with iced tea
Favourite drink: Mountain Dew
Favourite smell: CK One

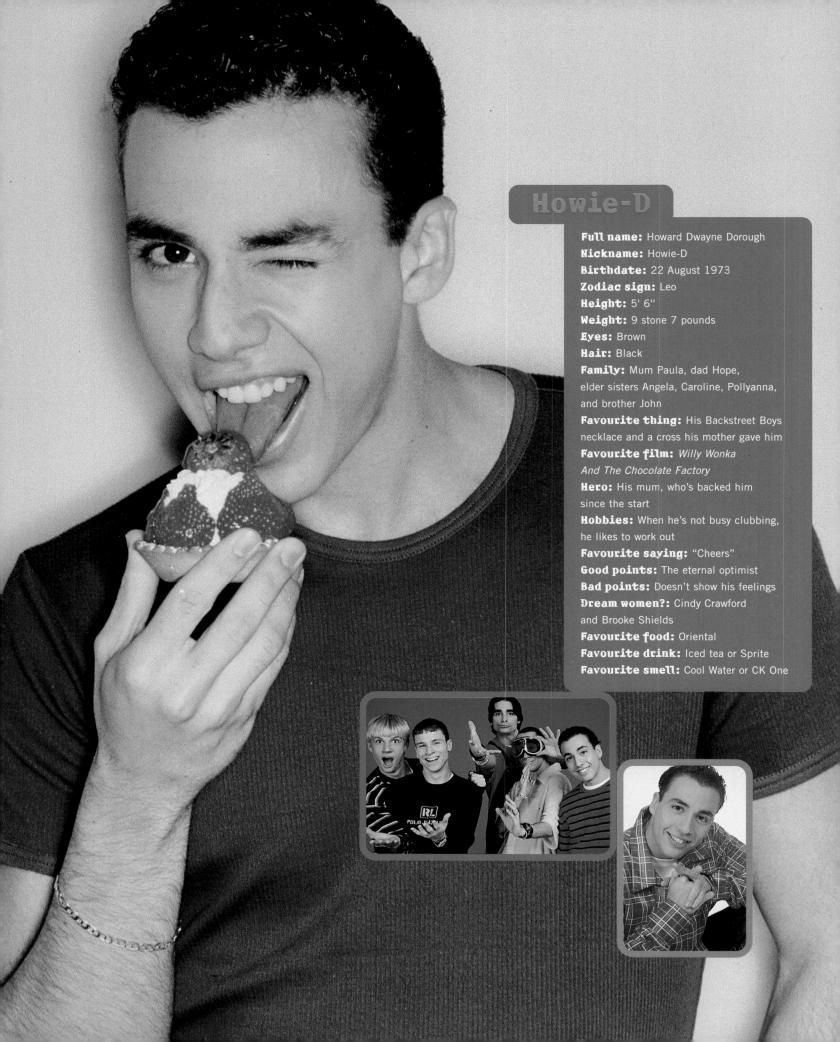

Howie-D

Full name: Howard Dwayne Dorough
Nickname: Howie-D
Birthdate: 22 August 1973
Zodiac sign: Leo
Height: 5' 6"
Weight: 9 stone 7 pounds
Eyes: Brown
Hair: Black
Family: Mum Paula, dad Hope, elder sisters Angela, Caroline, Pollyanna, and brother John
Favourite thing: His Backstreet Boys necklace and a cross his mother gave him
Favourite film: *Willy Wonka And The Chocolate Factory*
Hero: His mum, who's backed him since the start
Hobbies: When he's not busy clubbing, he likes to work out
Favourite saying: "Cheers"
Good points: The eternal optimist
Bad points: Doesn't show his feelings
Dream women?: Cindy Crawford and Brooke Shields
Favourite food: Oriental
Favourite drink: Iced tea or Sprite
Favourite smell: Cool Water or CK One

Nick

Full name: Nicholas Gene Carter
Born: Jamestown, New York
Nickname: Nick
Birthdate: 28 January 1980
Zodiac sign: Aquarius
Height: 5' 11" 'and still growing!'
Weight: 10 stone
Eyes: Blue
Hair: Blond
Family: Mum Jane and dad Robert, twins Aran and Angel, sister Lesley and brother BJ
Hero: Film director Ridley Scott
Favourite colour: Green
Hobbies: Playing Nintendo
Favourite saying: "It's all good!"
Good points: Considerate
Bad points: Obsessional: can take things that bit too far
Dream women?: Cindy Crawford and Sharon Stone
Favourite food: Pizza
Favourite drink: Coca Cola!

B-Rok

Full name: Brian Thomas Littrell
Nickname: B-Rok
Born: Lexington, Kentucky
Birthdate: 20 February 1975
Zodiac sign: Pisces
Height: 5' 8"
Weight: 10 stone
Eyes: Blue
Hair: Brown
Family: Mum Jackie, dad Harold, older brother Harold Baker Littrell III
Heroes: Boys II Men and Luther Vandross
Biggest fear: Heights
Hobbies: Going to the movies
Favourite saying: 'I guess'
Good points: The peacemaker of the band
Bad points: Still bites his nails!
Dream women?: Just one – Pamela Anderson
Favourite food: Macaroni and cheese
Favourite drink: Iced tea
Favourite smell: Photo by Lagerfeld

"I remember once we were performing a song from the album on stage and I had to sing the first two verses. The dance routine was really difficult and I was concentrating so hard I blanked on the words. I ended up just humming along. The other guys were useless. They were creased up laughing and didn't try to help me out at all!"
Brian

"I had my first kiss when I was four and kissed my next-door neighbour's daughter. Her name was Jennifer and then I ran away."
AJ

"When you're on the road it's difficult to keep up with the laundry so you find yourself without a clean pair of underpants. You have no choice but to pop back on yesterday's pair. They tend to be pretty snug, though, which is lucky."
Kev

"I used to stand on a tree stump in our back garden and sing, pretending the flowers were my audience. One day my mum caught me and enrolled me in singing lessons straight away."
Nick

"I like funny girls who will pop in and say, 'Here I am!' It doesn't matter what she looks like, though – honestly!"
AJ

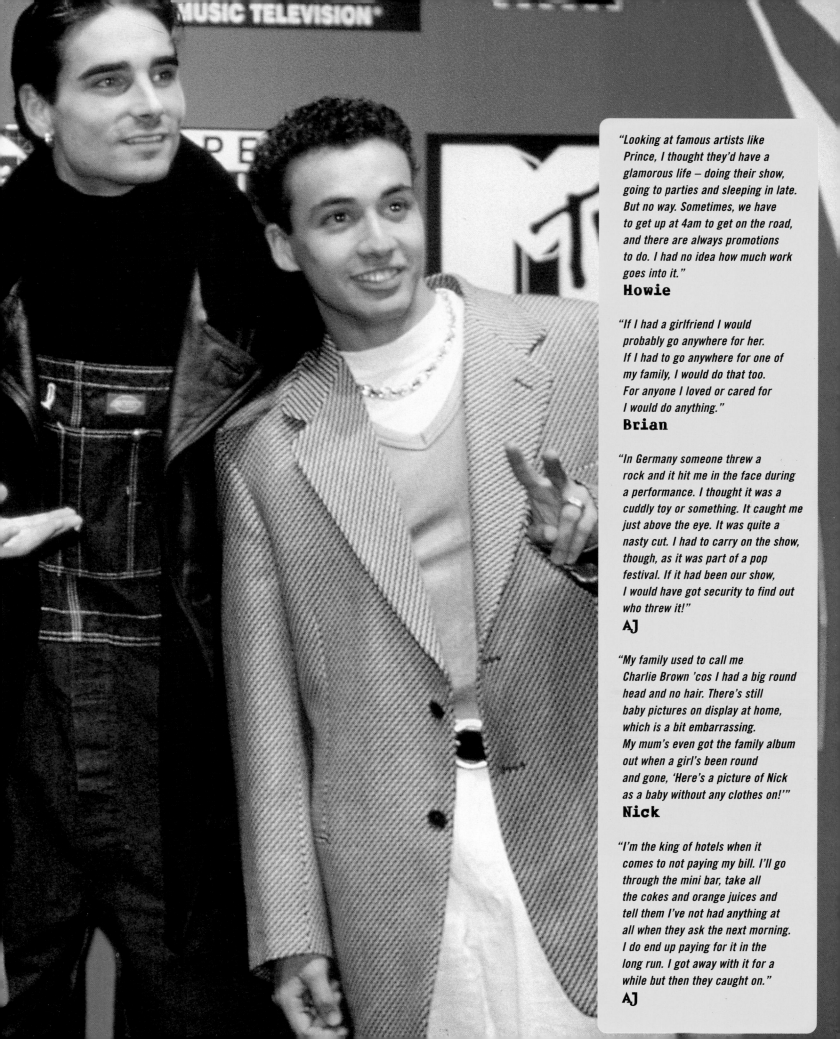

"Looking at famous artists like Prince, I thought they'd have a glamorous life – doing their show, going to parties and sleeping in late. But no way. Sometimes, we have to get up at 4am to get on the road, and there are always promotions to do. I had no idea how much work goes into it."
Howie

"If I had a girlfriend I would probably go anywhere for her. If I had to go anywhere for one of my family, I would do that too. For anyone I loved or cared for I would do anything."
Brian

"In Germany someone threw a rock and it hit me in the face during a performance. I thought it was a cuddly toy or something. It caught me just above the eye. It was quite a nasty cut. I had to carry on the show, though, as it was part of a pop festival. If it had been our show, I would have got security to find out who threw it!"
AJ

"My family used to call me Charlie Brown 'cos I had a big round head and no hair. There's still baby pictures on display at home, which is a bit embarrassing. My mum's even got the family album out when a girl's been round and gone, 'Here's a picture of Nick as a baby without any clothes on!'"
Nick

"I'm the king of hotels when it comes to not paying my bill. I'll go through the mini bar, take all the cokes and orange juices and tell them I've not had anything at all when they ask the next morning. I do end up paying for it in the long run. I got away with it for a while but then they caught on."
AJ

"I take the mickey out of Howie because it takes so long for him to do everything. And Kevin, 'cos he's the oldest – if he doesn't laugh with us, we say 'You're too much of an old man to understand our jokes.'"
Brian

"We did this live show at this radio station in Spain and when we came out, we were mobbed. I had a necklace on that meant a great deal to me – my brother gave it to me one Christmas – and this girl just ripped it off my neck!"
Kev

"My room at home is real tidy at the moment because I'm away. My keyboards are there, lots of Stephen King books and my sound system."
AJ

"When we picked the name Backstreet Boys we intended it to last forever. When we get older, when we grow up, we're gonna keep it, like The Beach Boys did, y'know. If we felt it was necessary we could drop the Boys and call ourselves Backstreet."
Brian

"I was asked out by girls a bunch of times when I was at school. I like girls asking you out because it takes the pressure off you having to do it, but it hasn't happened for a while, I'm sad to say!"
Nick

"My ideal Saturday night would be to go to the park, play some basketball for an hour until it gets dark then go back and have a shower at my house. After that I'd go and pick up a friend, not anyone in particular, and go to the movies, or out for dinner like a date."
Brian

"'We've Got It Goin' On' has a lot of good memories for me, 'cos it was our first single, which of course, we re-released in the UK. The first time we went to Europe was to promote this."
Kev

"We've got some brilliant fans. We get really excited when we're flying back into a country like Britain, because we get to meet them again – we literally sit on the plane going, 'Oh, do you think Helen, or Louise, or whoever, will be at the airport?'"
Brian

"We had a lot of fun recording 'Get Down (You're The One For Me)' at Fun Factory! Toni the producer was really cool, a great writer. I think it shows we can rap a little bit, and it has more of that hip-hop sound."
AJ

"I once put someone's name on the Statue of Liberty. I was going up a spiral staircase that led to the top and I saw everybody else's name and thought, 'What the heck?' It was mine and somebody else's name in a heart, but I'm not gonna kiss and tell."
Howie

"'Just To Be Close To You' is a percappella song – it's like cappella. Our voices make the music but it also has the drum track – it was very simple. It talks about being close and how that's what matters in the long run."
Brian

"I've never been drunk. I'm under age, so I'd get myself in trouble if I drank. It's never interested me. I've heard from some people that drinking isn't bad for your health if you keep it in moderation, but personally I don't like it."
Nick

"I'd like to be President for a day, just to see what it would be like in his shoes. What laws would I pass? Erm, I think there needs to be money put into cancer and AIDS research, especially since my dad died of cancer. I'd just use the money they had for better things."
Kev

"We're really focused on not taking our fans for granted. You can't get caught up with it, because there is no way to please everybody. But when we can, we like to give them some special attention. We're just trying to be nice and give a little something back."
AJ

"If we've been to see a scary movie or something and we're sharing a room, and the lights are off when we walk in Nick will go (whispering) 'It's dark in here isn't it?' And he's not being funny — he means it!"
Brian

"I've always loved flying. In high school, I was always debating whether to go to college, or to follow my dream into entertainment, or whether to go to the air force to become a pilot. I've had flying lessons but I've never been up in a helicopter."
Kev

"When I'm on the road the thing I miss most is sleeping in my own bed. When I get home I love sinking into my own sheets. I miss my pillow and duvet. Hotels are really uncomfortable. They're are either too hard or way too soft."
Brian

"If a girl's too loud and tries to get too much attention it kinda puts me off a little bit. And if they don't have very good manners, or if I hear them swearing, then that turns me off too."
Kev

"I'd love to get my eyebrow pierced and get three tattoos done. I'd have one on my back between my shoulder blades — a sun about as big as three Coke cans. Then, on my left arm, my nickname, 'Bone', and on my right arm a Japanese symbol/word meaning 'Eternal Life'."
AJ

"I have two scars where I had my appendix taken out, but only the people who know me really well get to see them 'cos they're at the bottom of my tummy! I've also got a scar on my head where I head-butted a table when I was 12."
Brian

"I'll never hang my feet off the end of the bed – I'm afraid little gremlins will bite my toes! Really!"
Nick

"My first kiss was with a girl called Gina Davison who I went to school with. I was in fifth grade. She was nice. That was my first real kiss."
Kev

"We've wanted to get back to the UK for a long time now, but what we want people to realise is that we're trying to conquer the whole world and that means we have to visit all these different countries. Unfortunately it doesn't leave us much time in each place, but what I want everyone to realise is that the fans have always been, and always will be the most important thing. After all, we'd be nothing without them."
Brian

"The most expensive thing I've ever bought is a gold chain that 'cost $300. I bought it for myself. How come I haven't bought a flash car and a house? Well, I haven't got a driving licence, and I'd rather stay at home with my parents."
Nick

"My room at home is very empty! I've just moved into an apartment with Howie and Brian. My room is decorated black and white."
Kev